During reading

- Encourage your child to describe what is going on in the pictures.

- Ask your child what is happening, and what they think might happen next.

- When you turn the page to see what actually happens, the outcome may or may not be what you expect! Talk about it.

- Give them lots of praise as you go along!

After reading

- Look at the back for some fun activities.

OXFORD
UNIVERSITY PRESS

Great Clarendon Street, Oxford OX2 6DP
Oxford University Press is a department of the University of Oxford.
It furthers the University's objective of excellence in research, scholarship,
and education by publishing worldwide. Oxford is a registered trade mark
of Oxford University Press in the UK and in certain other countries

First published 2022

British Library Cataloguing in Publication Data

Data available
ISBN: 978-0-19-278286-1

1 3 5 7 9 10 8 6 4 2

Printed in China

Paper used in the production of this book is a natural,
recyclable product made from wood grown in sustainable
forests. The manufacturing process conforms to the
environmentalbregulations of the country of origin.

TONY NEAL

TOO HEAVY, ELEPHANT!

OXFORD

UNIVERSITY PRESS

Can we play

on the
the
seesaw?

WHOOP!

Let's play
together!

You're too
heavy,
Elephant!

Climb on,
Mouse . . .

I'm too **heavy.**

And I'm too **light**.

But here comes
Rabbit . . .

3 2 1

Hop on board, Rabbit!

Still too
HEAVY!

Still too LIGHT!

Who's coming now?

3 2 1

It's Frog!

Still too light.
Climb up, Squirrel!

I'm going up!

DID IT!

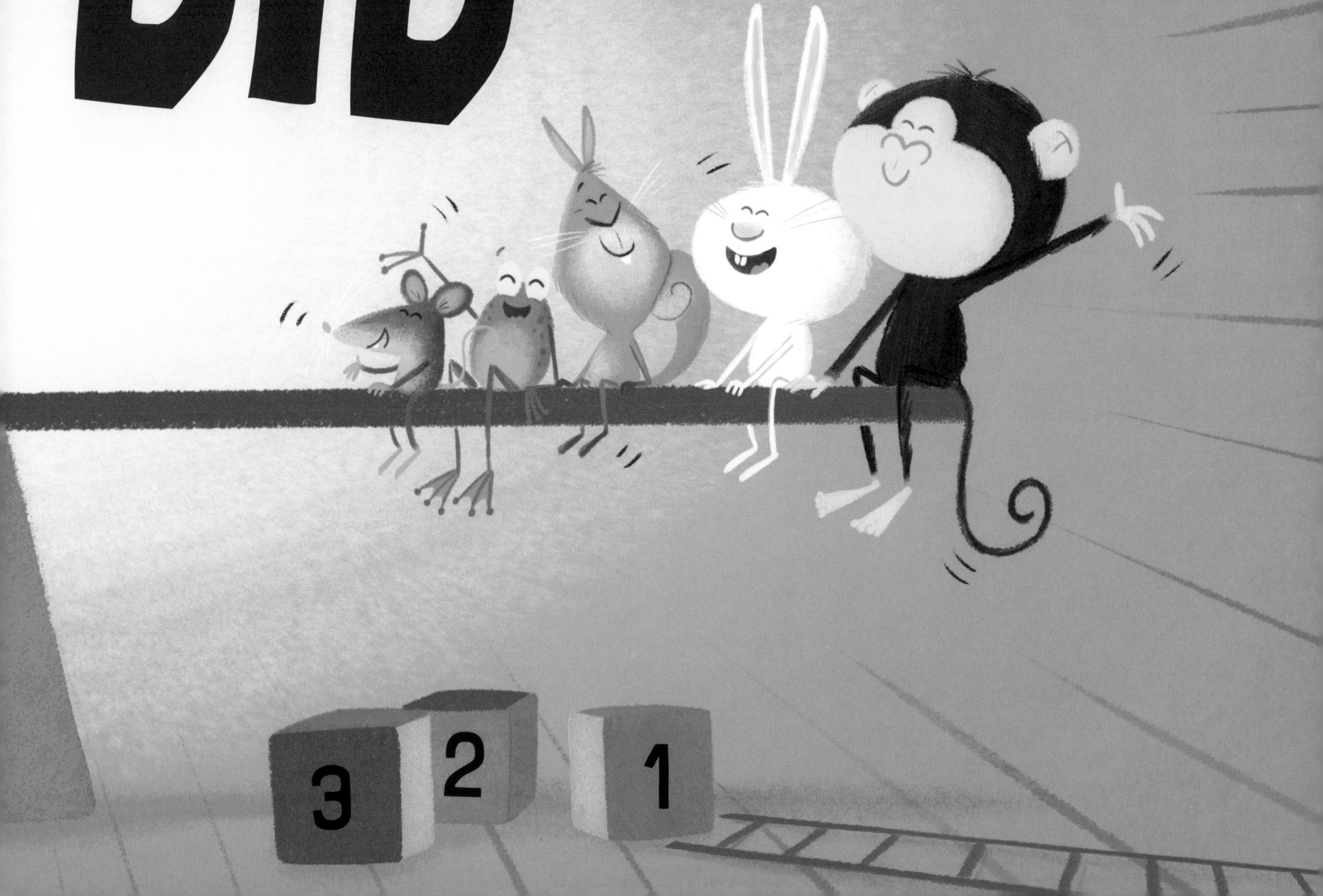

Activities

Heavy & Light

Guessing games

Gather a range of **heavy** and **light** objects from around your home, making sure they vary in **size**, **shape**, and **weight**. It is important that your items are obviously **heavy** or **light**.

e.g. a leaf, a crayon, a balloon, a bag of cotton wool, a full drink bottle, a big book

Without touching them, ask your child which items they think are **heavy**, and which they think are **light**.

Encourage your child to hold each object—do they still think it is **heavy** or **light**? Highlight **small** items that are **heavy**, and **large** items that are **light**.

Comparing weight

Fill small plastic cups with, for example, cotton wool, rice, and stones.

Challenge your child to work out which is the **heaviest** and which is the **lightest**, first just by looking.

Get your child to hold the pots and decide which is the **heaviest** and which is the **lightest**.

If you have scales you could **weigh** the pots together to check.

Vocabulary

heavy

heavier

heaviest

light

lighter

lightest